BLACKBIRCH PRESS, INC.
WOODBRIDGE, CONNECTICUT

Published by Blackbirch Press, Inc.
260 Amity Road
Woodbridge, CT 06525

First Edition

e-mail: staff@blackbirch.com
Web site: www.blackbirch.com

Printed in Singapore

10 9 8 7 6 5 4 3 2 1

Photo Credits
Cover: ©Corel Corporation, inset: ©B. Glassman; title page: ©B. Glassman; pages 4, 6, 7 (right), 10 (right): ©B. Glassman; pages 7 (left), 8, 9, 10 (left), 11-31: ©Corel Corporation.

Library of Congress Cataloging-in-Publication Data
Gresko, Marcia S.
Greece / by Marcia S. Gresko.
p. cm. — (Letters home from . . .)
Includes bibliographical references and index.
Summary: Describes some of the sights and experiences on a trip to Greece, including visits to Athens, Naxos, Mykonos, and Crete.
ISBN 1-56711-406-7
1. Gresco, Marcia S.—Journeys—Greece Juvenile literature. 2. Greece—Description and travel Juvenile literature. [1. Greece—Description and travel.] I. Title. II. Title: Letters home from—Greece III. Series.
DF728 .G745 1999 98-25618
914.9504'76—dc21 CIP

TABLE OF CONTENTS

Arrival in . . .

Athens

Yesterday we landed in Athens, the capital city of Greece. It's nice and warm and sunny here. Look on the map and you'll see that Greece is the southernmost country in Europe. It's a small, mountainous country, about the same size as the state of Alabama. But lots of big ideas were born here, like democracy and the Olympics. Our tour guide called Greece the "birthplace of civilization." That's because Greek traditions in government, art, science, medicine, and mathematics influenced many other cultures.

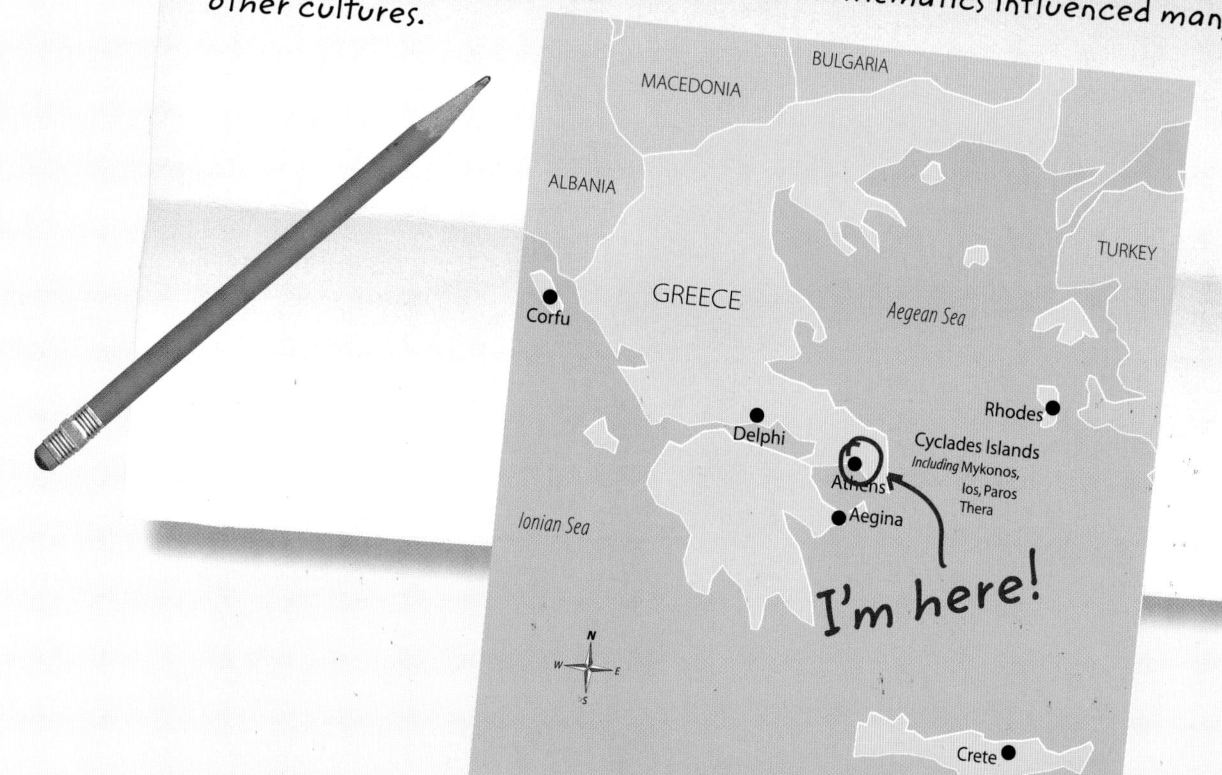

Modern Athens

Athens is a noisy, crowded city. Traffic jams made it faster to walk to most places instead of taking a taxi! More than half of all Greeks live in apartments in urban areas. And more people want to live in Athens than any other city in Greece. Every year, many Greeks move here from rural areas to look for jobs in the city's factories. Or, they work in the hotels, restaurants, and other businesses that serve the millions of tourists like us that visit the city each year.

Modern Athens is Greece's center of business and government. It is also the country's capital of education, culture, and entertainment. There are

Newsstands, Athens

Athens

important universities, impressive museums, peaceful parks, and many sports stadiums. Last night we went to the Athens Festival. It's a summer event that has musical and dance performances and plays.

Everywhere we went we saw reminders of the city's famous past. Ancient Athens had towering temples, grand theaters, and columned shopping centers about 2,000 years ago!

Our guide explained that Athens is like the statue of the Colossus—that's an enormous figure that was said to stand with one foot on either side of the harbor on the Greek island of Rhodes. Athens has one foot in the past and one foot ready to step into the next century!

Athens—History and Architecture

According to a legend our guide told us, God made Greece with leftover rocks after all the world's fertile soil had been used to make the rest of the countries.

People of ancient Greece lived in tribes, small kingdoms, and later in city-states. Each city-state was like a small country with its own economy, government, and religion. The city-states often went to war against each other. The two most powerful city-states were Sparta and Athens.

Athens was the richest city-state in Greece. During a 50-year period, known as the Golden Age, it was the center of Greek culture. Athens was also the birthplace of democracy. Its citizens were the first people in the world to vote for their own laws and leaders.

Parthenon

Hephaistos's Temple

Doric column, fortification walls

Ionic column, Acropolis

Corinthian columns near Corinth

The grand city was built on and around a flat-topped hill called the Acropolis, or high city. We climbed the ancient parade route that led to the top. That's where we saw Athens' most famous building—the Parthenon.

Temples like the Parthenon were the most important structures in Greece. Made of marble or stone, they were built with a long main room surrounded by columns. So far, I've learned that the Greeks had three styles of columns—simple Doric, graceful Ionic, and fancy Corinthian.

Greek temples were so beautiful that European and American architects copied them in many of their public buildings. The Lincoln Memorial in Washington, DC is one famous example.

Ancient Athens—Culture

Today we visited the Agora, a large open marketplace below the Acropolis.

The busy Agora was the center of Athenian daily life and culture. Farmers and craftsworkers sold everything from olives to fine painted pottery. Politicians met to debate government business. Philosophers like Socrates—who taught his students by asking questions—and scientists like Hippocrates—the "father of medicine"—gathered to discuss important ideas. They even had an athletic field there for competitions, and a theater for staging plays—a favorite Greek entertainment.

Ancient outdoor theater

Ancient Agora

Statue of Poseidon, National Archaelogical Museum

Entranceway to the original Olympic stadium

Temples to important gods also stood in the Agora. The Greeks worshipped many different gods and goddesses, but there were 12 main ones. These gods lived on Mount Olympus, the highest mountain in Greece. The most important god was Zeus. Poseidon was the god of the sea, Ares the god of war, Apollo the god of light and music. Important goddesses were Aphrodite the goddess of love, Athena the goddess of wisdom and war, and Artemis the goddess of the hunt. The Greeks told many stories, called myths, about the adventures of their gods.

The Greeks also held festivals in honor of their gods. The Olympic Games were held in honor of Zeus. The Games were so important that they even stopped wars in order to hold them!

Ios, Paros

This week we're traveling around Greece the way the ancient Greeks did—by boat.

Greece is a country of peninsulas and hundreds of islands. About 20% of Greece is made up of islands, so its people have always been good sailors.

Our boat traveled southeast from Athens to our first stop in the Cyclades Islands. These are dry, mountainous islands. They form the largest of the four main island groups in Greece.

More visitors travel to the Cyclades than to any other Greek island group. In ancient days, they had lots of visitors, too. Merchants from Europe, Asia, and Africa traded with the islands' bustling towns.

Ios Harbor

Naxos

Fisherman in Paros

Naxos is the largest and most fertile of the islands. It also has some of the best scenery. There were green fields, groves of fruit and olive trees, and herds of livestock. We toured centuries-old cathedrals, pirate watch-towers, a castle, and Naxos's most famous landmark—a giant stone doorway that leads nowhere!

Naousa is the fishing village on Paros where we stayed. The town was celebrating a historic sea battle it fought against Turkey. Children were dressed in native costumes, and there was feasting and dancing. The day ended with 100 torch-lit boats sailing into the harbor. What a sight!

Mykonos

We arrived in Mykonos a few days ago. The boat was crowded with tourists from all over the world. Mykonos is one of the most popular of the Greek islands. (It's where the "jet set" hangs out!)

We've been having a great time. The island's golden sand makes great sandcastles, and the glassy, blue-green Aegean Sea is warm and calm.

Downtown Mykonos is a happening place. It's like a great big maze to wander around. Its narrow, winding streets were laid out to confuse pirates who often visited the island to meet their mates and draft new crew members. In the evening, crowds fill the town's restaurants and clubs. Above it all stand Mykonos's famous windmills, once used to grind corn.

Mykonos Harbor

A friendly Mykonos woman

Mykonos's windmills dominate the skyline

Today, we took a short ride on a small wooden boat, called a caique, to the tiny islet of Delos. Delos was the religious and political center of the Aegean civilizations for 1,000 years. Legend says that it was the birthplace of twin gods—Artemis, the goddess of the hunt, and Apollo, the god of light and reason. Most of Delos was covered in ruins: temples, a gymnasium, a stadium, and a theater.

Tomorrow we're going to visit some more of the island's sights. Legend says that there are giant rocks in the countryside that are the bones of giants slain by the hero Hercules!

Food

What did you eat for breakfast today—cereal, eggs, pancakes? We ate thick, soft pretzel-like bread in the shape of a bracelet! Street vendors on our way to the early morning market had huge baskets of them. Supermarkets are becoming more common, but most Greeks like to do their shopping at small stores and open-air markets.

At the market, stalls were piled high with fresh fruits and vegetables grown on the small farms of central Greece and several islands. There was also fresh meat, cheese, and tons of fish (great snapper!). With more than 9,000 miles of coastline, seafood is an important part of the Greek diet.

Columns in the olive grove, Olympia

Olive trees, Crete

Sheep graze on the high grass

Fresh catch from offshore

We bought the ingredients for a tasty Greek salad—plump tomatoes, cucumbers, a creamy, salty white cheese called feta (made from goat's milk), and tangy black olives. According to legend, the olive was created by the Greek goddess Athena. Greece is one of the world's largest producers of olives.

Greeks eat dinner late! At about ten o'clock we joined the crowd at one of the many tavernas. Those are inexpensive, family-style restaurants. Specialties included grilled lamb kebabs, grape leaves stuffed with meat and rice, all kinds of fish, and casseroles of meat and vegetables. We all ordered something different so we could share.

Religion

Today we joined the saint's day festival in the town where we're staying. Most Greeks belong to the Greek Orthodox Church. Nearly every village, town, and city has a patron saint who is its special protector. On the patron saint's day, everyone in the community takes time to honor him or her.

The church was crowded with people. Some wore traditional costumes. Others wore their holiday best. The priests we had seen in their everyday black robes and tall, round hats had changed into golden ones for the occasion.

Priest and boy

Chapel and bell tower

The church walls were covered with colorful icons, or holy pictures. Most of the service took place behind a screen that surrounded the altar. At the end of the service, the priest gave everyone who had the same name as the saint a special piece of holy bread. Then he said a special blessing to celebrate their name day.

Afterward, the priest led a procession through the town and there was lots of food, lively music, and dancing. The church bells rang all day to spread the word that a festival was going on.

Religion plays an important part in daily life. Priests bless newly planted fields and new business openings. The Greek flag has a white cross on it, and religion is taught in the public schools.

Rhodes

Besides beautiful beaches, this large island has a bunch of really cool temples, churches, and a 500-year old castle. The Castle of the Grand Masters and the other fortresses around the island were built by a group of knights who owned Rhodes for more than 200 years. There were also mosques, mansions, and a beautifully decorated (and still-working) public bath house. These are reminders of a time when Turkey (across the Mediterranean) ruled Greece.

The most famous landmark, the Colossus of Rhodes, can no longer be seen. The huge stone figure, the size of the Statue of Liberty, once stood in the harbor but was destroyed by an earthquake.

Harbor in Lindos, Rhodes

Crusader Castle

Turkish Domination

Rhodes is the only stop we're making in the Dodecanese island group. The Dodecanese are Greece's southeastern most territory. The islands are actually closer to Turkey than to mainland Greece.

Greece and Turkey, its neighbor to the east, have been rivals for thousands of years. One legendary battle occurred when a Greek queen was kidnapped by a Turkish prince. According to the story, the Greek army finally won the ten-year-long battle when it invaded by hiding inside a giant, hollow, wooden horse.

More than 2,000 years later, Turkish armies conquered most of Greece, ruling it for about 400 years. Finally, with the help of other European countries, the Greeks won independence for about half of their land. Most of the remaining land was returned to Greece after World War I.

Riding donkeys to the acropolis of Lindos

Crete

From Rhodes, we traveled about 240 miles southwest to Crete. Located in the middle of the Mediterranean Sea, Crete is the largest of the Greek islands.

Crete was the birthplace of the first important European civilization about 5,000 years ago.

The Minoan culture (named after King Minos) was based on agriculture and trade. Skilled artists made beautiful jewelry and fine pottery. Scholars developed a decimal system and Europe's first system of writing. But at its height, a very strange thing happened—the Minoan culture suddenly vanished! One theory is that they were wiped out by earthquakes and tidal waves caused by a volcanic explosion on the nearby island of Thera.

The Palace at Knossos

Plakias, Crete

Mountain village, Crete

Matala, southern Crete

We visited the Palace at Knossos to see how wealthy Minoan kings once lived. There were storerooms, offices, crafts workshops, and luxurious apartments decorated with wall paintings of Minoan life. They even had indoor plumbing! There was also a confusing maze of rooms and hallways. Bulls were pictured everywhere. Our guide reminded us that legend says King Minos kept the Minotaur, a monster that was half man and half bull, in a maze called a labyrinth.

We also took daytrips from our hotel in the port city of Iraklion, stopping in mountain villages and for picnics at the beach.

Thera (Santorini)

Sailing into Thera was awesome! The island, often called Santorini, is what remains of the rim of a giant, still-active volcano. As we sailed across the volcano's flooded center into the harbor, we could see shores covered in black, volcanic sand. As we docked, our guide told us the amazing story. Many believe that Thera is the legendary "lost continent" of Atlantis. According to legend, angry gods punished Atlantis's overly proud people by sinking the great continent in a single day, more than 3,000 years ago.

Oia, Island of Thera

Sponges sold at the wharf

From the landing area, we had to climb almost 600 broad steps to get to Fira, the capital. Parts of Fira are built right into the steep surrounding cliffs.

One day we toured the newly uncovered ruins of a grand town buried by the volcano's eruption. Fine buildings and a sewer system tell archaeologists that an advanced civilization once lived here.

But, the best part of our stay was our boat ride to the Burnt Isles, two smoking cones in the middle of the bay. Thera has erupted four times during this century. The last time was less than 50 years ago, so I was a little nervous. But it was so cool to be standing right in the middle of an active volcano!

Corfu

We traveled northwest around Greece's hand-shaped Peloponnesian Peninsula to Corfu in the Ionian Sea.

Corfu and the rest of the seven islands in the Ionian island group are located off the west coast of Greece. Corfu is closer to Albania and Italy than it is to Athens. The island was ruled by Venice, a powerful Italian city-state, for about 400 years.

Countryside café in Corfu

Corfu and the Ionian Sea

In the countryside, fertile green Corfu was very different from the mostly bare, rocky landscapes on the Aegean islands. The Ionians get more rain than other islands. The hills were covered with groves of figs, oranges, and olives. There are about 20 times more olive trees on Corfu than there are people on all of the Ionian islands!

Our guide said that many people think Corfu is the magical island that the famous playwright William Shakespeare wrote about in one of his plays. From the friendly people we met and the beautiful scenery we enjoyed, I think they are right!

Delphi

From Corfu, we returned to the mainland to visit Delphi in central Greece.

Delphi is located on the steep, misty slopes of Mount Parnassus. That was supposedly the favorite hangout of the god Apollo, and of the Muses, goddesses who looked after art and music. Sacred to all Greeks, Delphi was thought to be the very center of the world.

Delphi

A huge temple complex was built on the sacred spot. Greeks made pilgrimages, or holy trips, here for more than 1,000 years. Most people came to the Temple of Apollo. Here they asked a priestess, called an oracle, for advice of all kinds.

The oracle was usually an older peasant woman with no special training. She would go into a trance and, inspired by Apollo, answer questions about the future. Her words were frequently spoken in riddles that made no sense to ordinary people. They had to be interpreted by the priests of the temple. But the Greeks took her predictions very seriously, and leaders consulted her before making important decisions like going off to war.

Aegina

We spent our last weekend in Greece on the island of Aegina. Because it's just a short ferry ride from Athens, it's a favorite weekend resort for families from the big city.

More than 2,600 years ago, Aegina became the first place in Europe to mint its own coins—silver with the image of a turtle stamped on them.

Aphaia Temple

An anchored schooner, Aegina

In modern times, Aegina's location made it an important base in the country's War of Independence. After the war, it was the first capital of the newly free nation, until the government was moved to Athens. Greece's first money, newspapers, and books were printed in Aegina.

Today, the island is famous for its tasty pistachio nuts. Farmers gently knock them from the trees with sticks, remove the shells, and soak them in sea water. Then they dry them on flat roofs and terraces all over the island. I'm bringing back a suitcase full to share!

Glossary

Civilization the advanced stage of human organization, technology, and culture.

Democracy a way of governing a country in which the people choose their leaders in elections.

Fertile a condition of soil that is good for growing crops.

Islet a small island.

Labyrinth a maze of confusing passageways.

Pilgrimage a journey to worship at a holy place.

Ruins the remains of something that had collapsed or been destroyed.

Rural the less-populated countryside.

Urban a highly populated city area.

For More Information

Books

Allard, Denise. *Greece* (Postcards From). Chatham, NJ: Raintree/Steck Vaughn, 1997.

MacDonald, Fiona. *I Wonder Why Greeks Built Temples and Other Questions About Ancient Greece* (I Wonder Why Series). Las Vegas, NV: Kingfisher Books, 1997.

Pearson, Anne. Nick Nicholls (Photographer). *Ancient Greece* (Eyewitness Books). New York, NY: Knopf, 1992.

Vaughan, Jenny. Donna Bailey. *Greece* (Where We Live). Chatham, NJ: Steck-Vaughn Library Division, 1990.

Web Site

The Ancient Olympics

Tour ancient Olympia and learn about the first Olympic Games—olympics.tufts.edu.

Index